My First Riddle

The South

Edited by Bobby Tobolik

First published in Great Britain in 2010 by:

Young Writers

Young Writers
Remus House
Coltsfoot Drive
Peterborough
PE2 9JX
Telephone: 01733 890066
Website: www.youngwriters.co.uk

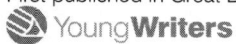

Foreword

'My First Riddle' was a competition specifically designed for Key Stage 1 children. The simple, fun form of the riddle gives even the youngest and least confident writers the chance to become interested in poetry by giving them a framework within which to shape their ideas. As well as this it also allows older children to let their creativity flow as much as possible, encouraging the use of simile and descriptive language.

Given the young age of the entrants, we have tried to include as many poems as possible. We believe that seeing their work in print will inspire a love of reading and writing and give these young poets the confidence to develop their skills in the future.

Our defining aim at Young Writers is to foster the talent of the next generation of authors. We are proud to present this latest collection of anthologies and hope you agree that they are an excellent showcase of young writing talent.

Contents

Woodborough CE (A) Primary School, Woodborough

The Poems

A Football Player

A football player
He is summer
He is a football court
He is a red football outfit
A big football
Football show
Popcorn.

Shania Kapoor

Food Riddle

I am brown and creamy
I am nice with chocolate sauce
And sprinkles and Smarties.
What am I?
Ice cream.

Harry Pegler (6)
Amberley Parochial School, Stroud

1

Food Riddle

I am squashy.
I am round.
I am spotty.
What am I?
I am an orange.

Angus Trippett (6)
Amberley Parochial School, Stroud

Food Riddle

I am delicious with custard.
I am smooth and sugary.
I can come from the shop or I can be home-made.
I can be at parties.
I can come in all sorts of colours.
I am lovely with a drink.
What am I?
Jelly.

Jack Pegler (7)
Amberley Parochial School, Stroud

Food Riddle

I am black and red and chewy.
I live in a box.
What am I?

Thomas Seare (5)
Amberley Parochial School, Stroud

My Friend, Robbie

He is faster than a cheetah.
He is a cool person.
His smile lights up the sky.
He is as cheeky as a monkey.
He is my friend, Robbie.

Callum Fulcher (6)
Clipstone Brook Lower School, Leighton Buzzard

Rey Mysterio

He is as cool as a tiger
He is as strong as an elephant
He is as fast as a monkey
He is Rey Mysterio.

Arron Dimmock (7)
Clipstone Brook Lower School, Leighton Buzzard

My Cat, Cecil

He is as big as a baby tiger.
He is as cute as a baby monkey.
He is as nice as a kitten.
He is Cecil, my cat.

Eleanor Sizeland (6)
Clipstone Brook Lower School, Leighton Buzzard

Hannah Montana

She has beautiful hair like an angel.
She is as gorgeous as a pop star.
She is as cuddly as a teddy.
She stands out in front of a crowd.
She is Hannah Montana.

Emily Kaye (6)
Clipstone Brook Lower School, Leighton Buzzard

My Friend, Emily

She is as fast as a cheetah,
She's as funny as a monkey,
She is as playful as a kitten,
She is my friend, Emily.

Mia Amsden Jane Doherty (7)
Clipstone Brook Lower School, Leighton Buzzard

My Dog, Tesse

He is lovely and ginger like a tiger.
He is as funny as a monkey.
He loves having a walk like children in school.
He is as cute as a tiny baby.
He is my dog, Tesse.

Tyrese Tarbot (7)
Clipstone Brook Lower School, Leighton Buzzard

Hannah Montana

She is as beautiful as a flower
She is as pretty as a princess
She is as cool as my friend
She is a good singer like a bird
She is Hannah Montana.

Georgia Blackstock (6)
Clipstone Brook Lower School, Leighton Buzzard

Whale Shark

It's like a zooming speedboat.
It eats fish every second.
It eats any kind of fish.
It's as big as a monster truck.
It's grey like mashed up snow.
It's a whale shark.

Joshua Hill (6)
Clipstone Brook Lower School, Leighton Buzzard

My Friend, Mia

She is like Rapunzel.
She sings beautifully, like a bird.
She moves gracefully, like a princess.
She swings on her chair, like a monkey.
She is as helpful as an elephant.
She is my friend, Mia.

Ben White (6)
Clipstone Brook Lower School, Leighton Buzzard

Cheetah

It's yellow and furry as a peach,
It's spotty, like a ladybird,
It has sharp teeth, like a lion,
It's as fast as a speedboat,
It's a speedy cheetah.

Alex Scorza (6)
Clipstone Brook Lower School, Leighton Buzzard

Hannah Montana

She is as graceful as a bird
She is like Rapunzel
She has beautiful hair, like the sun
She has wonderful clothes, like a colourful butterfly
She is Hannah Montana.

Paige Fowler (6)
Clipstone Brook Lower School, Leighton Buzzard

Gabriella

She is like a feather floating in the sky.
She is an excellent singer.
She has very long hair.
She is as light as a snowflake.
Twirling, swirling through the sky.
She is Gabriella.

Emily Dundas (6)
Clipstone Brook Lower School, Leighton Buzzard

My Bear

He is as cute as a bird.
He is as pretty as a dolphin.
He is as crazy as a football player.
He is as lovely as a rose.
He is my bear.

Tegan Shaw (6)
Clipstone Brook Lower School, Leighton Buzzard

My Mum

She is as small as a flower
She is as nice as a rose
She is as lovely as a dolphin
She is as caring as an angel
She is my mum.

Abigail Ham (7)
Clipstone Brook Lower School, Leighton Buzzard

My Dear Brother

He is as handsome as a prince,
He is as funny as a clown,
He is as clever as a tortoise,
He is as caring as a mother,
He is as cool as an ice cube,
He is as cheeky as a monkey,
He is as chubby as a cheek,
He is as strong as a buffalo,
He is as playful as a cat,
He is my wonderful, dear brother, Ahmad.

Aishah Salihu (7)
Cranfield (VC) Lower School, Bedford

Who Is Green And Grumpy?

He is as green as the grass,
He is stronger than the wind,
He can growl louder than a bear,
He can tear through anything,
He is bigger than my dad,
He can get very mad,
He is the Incredible Hulk.

Jacob Griffiths (5)
Cranfield (VC) Lower School, Bedford

Tiny

He is as fluffy as a pompom
He is soft like a pillow
He is smart like my dad
I can make him dance like Michael Jackson
He is cuddly like my mummy
He is like my best friend
He is my favourite teddy . . . Tiny.

Kira Palmer (7)
Cranfield (VC) Lower School, Bedford

Shark

I am feared because I am misunderstood.
My family has been alive since the mesozoic era.
I did not die out when the dinosaurs disappeared.
I have no scales, but I am a fish.
I have no bones, but a strong and flexible skeleton.
I am streamlined, fast and deadly but also quite shy.
My name can be Angel, Thresher, Basking or White-tip.
I am a shark.

Stephen Nitaan Simmons (6)
Cranfield (VC) Lower School, Bedford

My Brother, Joe

He is as small as a mouse.
He is as cute as a kitten.
He cries louder than a trumpet.
He cuddles like a koala.
He is my baby brother, Joseph.

Bethany Bociek (6)
Cranfield (VC) Lower School, Bedford

Emily

She has hair the colour of wheat,
She is really sweet,
She has a big smile,
She plays with me,
She is my very best friend,
She is Emily.

Harvey West (5)
Cranfield (VC) Lower School, Bedford

My Favourite Fruit

I am juicy and yummy
You can eat me
You can drink me
I am a colour
What am I?
An orange.

Lucas Manning (6)
Cranfield (VC) Lower School, Bedford

Shark

It is faster than an elephant,
It is as fierce as a dinosaur,
It can live in a sea cave,
It eats meat.
It is a shark.

William Cameron (6)
Dinton CE Primary School, Dinton

Lion

It can catch its prey,
It is as fast as a cheetah,
It is as camouflaged as the grass,
It lives in Africa.
It is a lion.

Toby Knight (6)
Dinton CE Primary School, Dinton

Dolphin

It can jump six metres above the water,
It's as clever as a sportsman,
It's as nice as an orca giving its baby some food,
It can jump higher than a mouse,
It's the best animal in the world,
It's a dolphin!

Jody Scott (6)
Dinton CE Primary School, Dinton

Snake

It is as slithery as a snail,
It likes to live in the dark,
It likes to eat mice,
It's got gummy teeth,
It is a snake.

Molly McCarthy (6)
Dinton CE Primary School, Dinton

Rabbit

It is whiter than the snow,
It can jump higher than a frog,
It is soft,
It is a rabbit.

Amber Hendrich (6)
Dinton CE Primary School, Dinton

Our Pig

It is slower than an elephant,
It is fatter than me,
It lives on a farm,
It is smaller than a cow,
It is a pig.

Tom Cook & Alex Collins (6)
Dinton CE Primary School, Dinton

Dog

It is softer than a cushion,
It eats biscuits,
It is faster than a cat,
It is cleverer than a cat,
It has sharp teeth,
It is a dog.

Louise Davies (6)
Dinton CE Primary School, Dinton

My Cat

It catches rats,
It runs fast like a dog,
It's funny as a clown,
It drinks water,
It's Bubble Sock, my cat.

Ben Lodge (7)
Dinton CE Primary School, Dinton

My Dog

It's like a cat,
It's furry like a horse,
It digs like a badger,
It's shiny like a star,
It's my dog, Oddie!

Chloe Yates (6)
Dinton CE Primary School, Dinton

T-Rex

Its teeth are as sharp as a razor
It's as smelly as a skunk
Its tail is as long as a snake
It eats other dinosaurs
It is a T-Rex.

Honey Webb (7)
Dinton CE Primary School, Dinton

My Aeroplane

It's as heavy as ten buses,
It flies as high as a giraffe,
It's as big as three elephants,
It has as many seats as a cinema,
It's as fast as the wind,
It's an aeroplane.

Orla Lovatt-Williams (6)
Dinton CE Primary School, Dinton

Eagle

It's as fast as a car
It dives in the water
It lives in the mountains
Their claws are as sharp as a tooth
Their wings are as big as me
It's an eagle.

James Nuttall (6)
Dinton CE Primary School, Dinton

The Skunk

It's as bright as a white wall,
It's as black and white as an old movie,
They live in the forest like a bear,
It's as smelly as dinosaur poo,
It is a skunk.

Harvey Holder (6)
Dinton CE Primary School, Dinton

Dragon

It has two arms like a person,
It has claws as sharp as knives,
It flies as fast as a rocket,
It is as scary as a dinosaur.
What is it?
Dragon.

Dylan Potter (6)
Dinton CE Primary School, Dinton

My Gus

He is as furry as an elephant
He is littler than an elephant
He is as cute as an elephant
He is my guinea pig called Gus.

Freya Miller (6)
Dinton CE Primary School, Dinton

Untitled

I have four wheels
I have four windows
What am I?
A car.

Hafsha Shakoor (7)
Downside Infant School, Luton

Octopus

I have eight legs
I am all purple
I have two eyes
I live under the sea
What am I?
I am an octopus.

Aliyha Malik (7)
Downside Infant School, Luton

It Comes From The Moon

I love it,
You get it from the moon,
You love it,
The mice have got to have it too.

Ali Noble (6)
Downside Infant School, Luton

Untitled

I am tall
I have four long legs
I am tall enough to reach my food
I can carry lots of things
I can climb the rocky mounts
I eat lovely potatoes
What am I?

Amina Ali Garnit
Downside Infant School, Luton

A Fluid Riddle

I can be hot
I can be cool
I can be collected in a pool
What am I?
Water.

Zakariya Saqib (7)
Downside Infant School, Luton

Who Am I?

I have eight legs
I live in the sea
I am in a cave
Who am I?

Rameesha Mahmood (6)
Downside Infant School, Luton

Egg

I am white on the outside and
Yellow on the inside
What am I?

Amna Sajid (6)
Downside Infant School, Luton

Beginning Letter

What is at the beginning of eternity
And at the end of time and space?
The letter E.

Henna Watif (7)
Downside Infant School, Luton

Guess The Riddle

It has four legs
It is yellow and it has brown spots
It has one tail
It has a long neck
And it can run fast
And it has a mane
It eats twigs on trees
What is it?
Giraffe.

Saira Amar (6)
Downside Infant School, Luton

Superhero Riddle

He is red and blue,
But nobody knows he has a spider on his chest,
On his red and blue vest.
He will fight all night until everything is alright.
Have no fear, guess who is here?
It's Spider-Man.

Hasan Amer (6)
Downside Infant School, Luton

Ben 10

I fight bad people.
I can turn into ten different aliens.
I'm the hero of this town.
I have a watch.
I am ten.
Who am I?

Faizan Mehmood (6)
Downside Infant School, Luton

What Am I?

I have four legs and I eat grass.
I am yellow and I am black.
I do not like tigers.
I can touch the tree with my mouth.
What am I?
I am a giraffe.

Ehsaan Khan
Downside Infant School, Luton

What Am I?

I have four legs.
I am white and soft.
I have one tail,
Some whiskers,
Two ears and two eyes.
I love to eat carrots.
I am a rabbit.

Labiba Rahman (6)
Downside Infant School, Luton

My Mum

I am nice.
I take care of you.
I cook for you.
I take you to school.
When you are naughty I shout.
When you're ill I take care of you.
Who am I?

Fiza Khawar (6)
Downside Infant School, Luton

Zoom, Zoom

I am fast,
I am cool,
I have weird doors,
I have boosters,
Sometimes I am in a race,
I am running on autopilot.
What am I?
I am a Ferrari.

Wajeeh Shah (7)
Downside Infant School, Luton

Innocent Mind

I save people
I fight baddies
I save your life
I have a weapon
Who am I?
I am Bruce Lee.

Dhillon Ahmed (7)
Downside Infant School, Luton

Untitled

I like to run.
I like to catch things.
I like to play with you all day.
I bark when I see you.
What am I?
I am a dog.

Hasan Zahid (6)
Downside Infant School, Luton

What Am I?

I put out fire.
I wear leather fireproofs.
If there's a fire in a house I put it out.
If there's a flood I drain it out.
What am I?

Jamal Faiza Tanvir Frida (7)
Downside Infant School, Luton

What Am I?

I need to be in water.
I have to swim in water.
I eat lots of fish.
I am scared of whales.
I am bigger than a fish.
I have sharp teeth.
What am I?
I am a shark.

Asif Razaq (7)
Downside Infant School, Luton

Tiger

I have a big roar.
I am orange and white.
I can scare all the farm animals.
What am I?

Zarish (6)
Downside Infant School, Luton

Animals

I am mean,
I have four legs,
I can run fast,
I have eyes,
I am yellow,
I am spotty,
What am I?
I am a cheetah.

Mariam Sultana (7)
Downside Infant School, Luton

What Am I?

I am all grey.
Snakes and owls eat me.
People try to trap me.
I've got good hearing.
I come out at night-time.
I like to eat food.
I am so small.

Kiran Bahadar (7)
Downside Infant School, Luton

What Am I?

I have long hair.
I can run very fast.
I eat grass and nuts.
You can ride me.
When I am show jumping
People brush my hair and train me.
What am I?

Humaira Majid (6)
Downside Infant School, Luton

Untitled

I was born in a cocoon.
I come out in nice weather.
First I am a caterpillar.
I get in the cocoon and
When I get out I have wings.
I am brightly coloured.
What am I?

Adrijus Liaukevicius (7)
Downside Infant School, Luton

London Cage

My animal is long.
It is in a cage.
My animal is fat.
It is a bit wide.
What is it?

Hashim Ul-Haq (6)
Downside Infant School, Luton

Rabbits

They are small, cute and soft.
They bounce around.
They have big fluffy tails.
They can come in all colours
And they have big ears.
They have little legs and long feet.

Amna Rehman (7)
Downside Infant School, Luton

What Am I?

It is as thin as a piece of paper.
It is as wet as a bit of ice.
It is as shiny as a disco ball.
It is as fast as a cheetah.
It is as flappy as a penguin.
It is as smart as a lion.
It is as greedy as a dog.
It is as slippery as some mud.
What am I?

Ben Bayley (6)
Frenchay CE Primary School, Frenchay

What Am I?

It is as furry as a cheetah.
It is as cute as a cat.
It is as crazy as a jaguar.
It is as nice as a fish.
It is as sweet as a star.
It is as dozy as an elephant.
It is as kind as a tiger
What am I?

Abigail Beaumont (6)
Frenchay CE Primary School, Frenchay

What Am I?

It is as fast as a hare.
It is as cute as a rabbit.
It is as funny as a rabbit.
It is as smiley as a girl.
It is as fun as a cat.
It is as soft as a coat.
It is as happy as a smile.
It is as good as a kitten.
It is as playful as a baby.
It is as small as a frog.
It is a dog.

Millie Vero (6)
Frenchay CE Primary School, Frenchay

What Am I?

I eat meat like a crocodile.
I am as fit as a cheetah.
I have whiskers like a mouse.
What am I?
I am a lion.

Joe Redgers (5)
Frenchay CE Primary School, Frenchay

What Am I?

I am as black and yellow as a cheetah.
I am as little as a bead.
I have big wings.
I like flowers.
I am in hot countries like France.
I am as spiky as a hedgehog.
What am I?
Bee.

Avneet Bisla (6)
Frenchay CE Primary School, Frenchay

What Am I?

It is as smooth as a piece of fur.
It is as pretty as a fairy.
It is as beautiful as a feather.
It is as kind as a dog.
You can stroke them when you ride them.
What is it?

Emily Rosenberg (5)
Frenchay CE Primary School, Frenchay

Untitled

My teeth are big like a lion.
My markings are brown.
I can run as fast as a car.
I can run as fast as a motorbike.
I can run as fast as a lion.
My feet are small.
I'm scared of the gorilla.
If I'm in the zoo, I'm well scared.
I can run as fast as a racing car.

Mohammed Kordofani (6)
Frenchay CE Primary School, Frenchay

Untitled

They are as funny as a clown.
They are as naughty as a rabbit.
They sometimes cut you like a dog.
They are as weird as a tiger.
They are as fluffy as a chick.
They go for a walk on their own.
They are as fluffy as a feather.
They are as soft as a cushion.
They seek attention like dogs.
What are they?

Evie Cook (6)
Frenchay CE Primary School, Frenchay

Untitled

It is as tough as a giraffe.
It is as strong as a dog.
It can run as fast as a horse.
It has got dry skin like a tortoise.
What is it?

Mollie Musty (6)
Frenchay CE Primary School, Frenchay

What Am I?

It is as fluffy as a feather.
It hops higher than a kangaroo.
It is very funny and cuddly.
It is very small, like a hamster.
What am I?

Kiera Campho (6)
Frenchay CE Primary School, Frenchay

Fluffy Paws

My paws are as fluffy as a cat.
I am very sweet.
My ears are very floppy.
I have fur as soft as wool.
I am as helpful as a child.
I am sometimes mad.
I am very cute.
I am sometimes dangerous.
I am very silly.
I am playful.
I seek attention.
I am very strong.
What am I?

Phoebe McDowall (6)
Frenchay CE Primary School, Frenchay

What Am I?

It is as dirty as a rat,
It is as thin as a chick,
It is as fast as a dog,
It is as stinky as a rat,
It perches a lot,
It is as funny as a clown,
And sometimes it sits on eggs.
What is it?

Darcy Evans (6)
Frenchay CE Primary School, Frenchay

What Am I?

I swing like a skipping rope,
I swing on trees,
I am as furry as a teddy bear,
What am I?

Erin Green (5)
Frenchay CE Primary School, Frenchay

What Am I?

I have yellow hair like the sun.
I am mighty.
I can run as fast as a leopard.
I have whiskers like a cat.
What am I?

Summer Cepek (5)
Frenchay CE Primary School, Frenchay

A Cat

He is as fluffy as a cardigan,
He is as soft as a pillow,
He is as cute as a hamster,
He is as pointy as a flower,
He is as noisy as a tiger,
What is he?
He is a cat.

Rhianne Carrick (5)
Hadrian Lower School, Dunstable

Untitled

It is as clean as a car wash,
It is noisy like a jet,
It is as fast as a speedboat,
It is as cool as a quad bike,
What is it?
A motorbike.

Sam Mills (6)
Hadrian Lower School, Dunstable

A Motorbike

It is as clean as a car,
It is as shiny as a mirror,
It is as cool as a quad bike,
It is as noisy as a car,
What is it?
A motorbike.

Reece Drew (6)
Hadrian Lower School, Dunstable

A Person

Hair as long as string.
Eyes as shiny as glass.
Skin as light as the sun.
What am I?
A person.

Jamilah Mufaro Jawando (5)
Hadrian Lower School, Dunstable

A Cat

It is as soft as a pillow.
It is as cute as a bunny rabbit.
It is as noisy as a tiger.
It is as cuddly as can be.
What am I?
I am a cat.

Lilly Mae Dunlop-Marriott (6)
Hadrian Lower School, Dunstable

A Giraffe

As tall as a tree,
As brown as the sand,
As fast as a car,
As cheeky as a monkey,
I am a giraffe.

James Stewart (6)
Hadrian Lower School, Dunstable

SpongeBob

He is as yellow as the sun,
He is as silly as a jumping bean,
He is as wild as the waves,
He is as square as a TV.
He is SpongeBob.

Macey Herd (6)
Hadrian Lower School, Dunstable

Hannah's Rabbit

He is as bouncy as a kangaroo,
He is really fast and runs like a cheetah,
He wiggles like a worm,
He is as soft as silk,
He is Hannah's rabbit.

Daniel Meadows (6)
Hadrian Lower School, Dunstable

My Cat

As soft as a pillow,
As cuddly as Santa,
As sweet as a lolly,
As happy as me,
This is my cat.

Kate Yin Chan (6)
Hadrian Lower School, Dunstable

Libby

She is as bright as the sun in the sky,
She can sing like a robin,
She is as pretty as the sun,
She has nice earrings that sparkle like the stars,
It is Libby.

Leia Smith (6)
Hadrian Lower School, Dunstable

A Leopard

As fast as a Virgin plane,
As yellow as the sun,
As spotty as a ladybird,
As cunning as a fox,
It is a leopard.

Siddhant Deshmukh (5)
Hadrian Lower School, Dunstable

Goldy The Fish

I am as long as a little finger,
I am as shiny as tinsel,
I am as fast as a rabbit,
My mouth is like a tunnel,
I am Goldy the fish.

James Preston (6)
Hadrian Lower School, Dunstable

My Cat

As fast as a lion,
As orange as the sun,
As smooth as the window,
As shiny as jewels,
This is my cat.

Nisha Patel (5)
Hadrian Lower School, Dunstable

Wayne Rooney

He is as fast as lightning,
He dribbles as fast as a baby,
He shoots like an arrow,
He is as fit as a fiddle,
He is Wayne Rooney.

Jakob Ward (6)
Hadrian Lower School, Dunstable

My Mummy

She is as beautiful as a princess,
She is as funny as a monkey,
She has earrings that shine like a star,
She is as kind as a nurse,
She is my mummy.

Harriette Hewitt (6)
Hadrian Lower School, Dunstable

What Am I?

I have a squiggly body
And I am floating all the time.
I have shiny gold skin
And a bright gold flapping tail.
I am very, very scaly.
What am I?
A goldfish.

Alex England (7)
Hanwell Fields Community School, Banbury

What Am I?

I am big and fluffy.
I look like a parachute.
I am dangerous and fierce.
I live in the deep blue sea.
I am powerful.
I look like a mushroom.
What am I?
Jellyfish.

Oscar Gaynor (7)
Hanwell Fields Community School, Banbury

What Am I?

I am a big sea creature.
I have big bulgy eyes.
I am bright pink.
I can float up into the sea.
I have big wiggly, jiggly tentacles coming down.
I have big, soft skin.
I am a fierce creature that stings you.
I am really scary.
I am a mushroom floating in the sea.
Jellyfish.

Haridri Namesha Goonewardena (6)
Hanwell Fields Community School, Banbury

What Am I?

I live in beautiful rocks
I am dangerous
I can kill fish with my sharp teeth
I am very colourful
I am a very big ferocious thing
I have a sharp pointy fin
What am I?
A shark.

Cameron Blake (6)
Hanwell Fields Community School, Banbury

What Am I?

I live in the deep blue sea,
I am a fast swimmer,
I have some big, bumpy flippers,
I have a big, round, patterned shell,
I move slowly on land,
What am I?
A turtle.

Sophie Liggins (6)
Hanwell Fields Community School, Banbury

What Am I?

I have bobbly eyes
I dance very slowly in the sea
I swim very fast
I am beautiful
I live in the deep dark sea
I have lovely colours
I love people
I am friendly
I am dark green.

Sara Alia (6)
Hanwell Fields Community School, Banbury

What Am I?

I live in the deep dark sea
I move very fast
I twirl out of the sea
I have a silver shiny body
I jump high above the water
What am I?
A dolphin.

Freya Alexander (6)
Hanwell Fields Community School, Banbury

My Cat

She is as peaceful as a ballerina.
She is as fluffy as a teddy bear.
She is as calm as an angel.
She is as white as snow.
She is as sweet as an apple.
She is as cute as a bunny.
She is my cat.

Imogen Tredwell (7)
Harriers Ground Community Primary School, Banbury

Funny Hamster

He is as funny as a monkey.
He is as lovely as a banana,
He is as furry as a teddy,
He is as fast as a horse,
He is as fantastic as a rock climber,
He is as brilliant as a dancer.

Emily Vint (6)
Harriers Ground Community Primary School, Banbury

My Bunny

She is as cute as an apple.
She is as fluffy as a string of wool.
She is as white as a cloud.
She is as naughty as a parrot.
She is as soft as a pillow.
She is as light as a feather.

Cathryn Kirk (6)
Harriers Ground Community Primary School, Banbury

Dragon

He has got wings,
He can breathe fire.

Morgan Young (6)
Harriers Ground Community Primary School, Banbury

Giraffe

It has a long neck.
It has long legs.
It can reach branches.
It can eat leaves off the trees.

Chloe Crane (7)
Harriers Ground Community Primary School, Banbury

Lion

It is rich,
It has a mane,
It can roar.

Felix Adams (5)
Harriers Ground Community Primary School, Banbury

Harvey

He is as annoying as a devil,
He is as chubby as a hamster,
He is as funny as a clown,
He is as fidgety as a bee,
He is as speedy as lightning,
He is as naughty as a bull,
Who is he?

Harry Allen (5)
Harriers Ground Community Primary School, Banbury

Which Fairy Tale Character Am I?

I have a blue dress.
My lips are red as roses.
My hair is as gold as toast.
I have a dog called Toto.
I fall asleep in flowers.
My house flew to a colourful land.
Who am I?

Abigail Roskilly (6)
Middleton Cheney Community Primary School, Banbury

Which Fairy Tale Character Am I?

I have blonde hair like the sun,
I lost some things,
I live with my evil stepmother,
I marry a prince,
My stepmother tricks me,
Even my sisters are nasty.
Who am I?

Zoe Marsh (6)
Middleton Cheney Community Primary School, Banbury

Which Fairy Tale Character Am I?

I live with my mum
I climbed a beanstalk
There was a castle
'Fi fi fo fum'
Who am I?

Charlie Van Santen (6)
Middleton Cheney Community Primary School, Banbury

Which Fairy Tale Character Am I?

My house is strong,
My friends run to my house because there is somebody chasing them,
He knocks on the door,
We don't let him in,
He goes down the chimney,
He falls in a pot,
Who am I?

Kelly Newman (7)
Middleton Cheney Community Primary School, Banbury

Which Famous Person Am I?

He has hair as black as the night
His singing is better than a robin
He is more handsome than a prince
He knows how to play the guitar and piano
His nickname is 'The King'.
Elvis.

Leigh-Ann Rippon (7)
Middleton Cheney Community Primary School, Banbury

Who Are We?

They are four fantastic singers,
They are dazzling dancers,
They sing like birds on a roof,
Their name begins with J.
JLS.

Jacob Large (6)
Middleton Cheney Community Primary School, Banbury

Who Am I?

He is a famous singer
He can moonwalk like an astronaut
He sings as loud as he can
He wears a glove that sparkles like a diamond
He wears a hat as black as the night
He has long and curly hair, like a girl
I'm bad, I'm bad, I'm really, really bad.
Michael Jackson

Tyler-Jade Prosser (7)
Middleton Cheney Community Primary School, Banbury

A Riddle

It is as soft as a teddy
It is as soft as a mouse
It is as cute as a kitten
It is as sweet as a flower
It is as pretty as a doll
It is as yellow as a lemon
It is as gorgeous as a newborn baby
It is as nice as a puppy
It is as kind as a friend
It is a chick on a farm.

Katrina Robinson (7)
Prior Park Pre-Prep School, Cricklade

A Riddle

She is as kind as a bird.
She is better than a monkey.
She is as pretty as can be.
She is nice like my teacher.
She looks beautiful.
She is my friend, Evi.

Niki Erfanmanesh (7)
Prior Park Pre-Prep School, Cricklade

A Riddle

He is a good singer.
He likes being in fashion.
He sings funky songs.
He is good.
He is a good listener.
He is as fast as the wind.
He can do tricks.
He is big.
He is brainy.
He can do lots of things.

Ben Wilson (6)
Prior Park Pre-Prep School, Cricklade

A Riddle

She is as soft as a bunny,
She is as cheeky as a monkey.
She is as cuddly as a teddy bear.
She is happier than a chick.
She is as lovely as a flower.
She is as cool as an ice cream.
She is my mummy.

Paige Walton (6)
Prior Park Pre-Prep School, Cricklade

A Riddle

He is as fast as a cheetah.
He is very smart.
He is a good listener.
He can do very much.
He is very good at fighting.
He has a plan before he does anything.
He is very smart.
He is my friend Jerry the mouse.

Jubril-Deen-Amzart (6)
Prior Park Pre-Prep School, Cricklade

A Riddle

She is better at singing than my dad
She is better at the flute than me
She is older than me
She is taller than my mum
She is better at dancing than Cheryl Cole
She is sweeter than a sugar plum
She is prettier than a flower
She is my sister, Avani.

Kimiya Lal (6)
Prior Park Pre-Prep School, Cricklade

A Riddle

He was as black as a bear
He was kinder than my mum
He was a pop star
He could dance better than my dad
He was arrested lots of times
He died at fifty
He was more handsome than JLS
He was cooler than Lionel Richie
He was richer than Hannah Montana
He was braver at singing than my nanny
He was Michael Jackson.

Michael Austen (7)
Prior Park Pre-Prep School, Cricklade

A Riddle

She is as sweet as a robin,
She is as beautiful as a fish,
She is as thin as a giraffe,
She sings like a bird,
She is Leona Lewis.

Abigail Knight (6)
Prior Park Pre-Prep School, Cricklade

A Riddle

It is as fast as the wind
Its eyes are as dark as the night
It is as strong as a gorilla
It is as big as a jaguar
It is as fierce as a monster
It has a hiss as loud as a snake
Its teeth are as big as a sabre-tooth cat
It is as yellow as the sun.
It is a leopard.

Luca Railton (6)
Prior Park Pre-Prep School, Cricklade

A Riddle

He is as mad as a Mad Hatter,
He is as smiley as a cheetah,
He is as handsome as a prince,
He is as good as gold,
He is Captain Adorable.

Amelie Daniels (6)
Prior Park Pre-Prep School, Cricklade

A Riddle

She can sing like a robin,
She is as sweet as a dolphin,
She has long hair like Cheryl Cole,
She is cute like a rabbit,
She is Hannah Montana.

Meghan Williams (7)
Prior Park Pre-Prep School, Cricklade

A Riddle

She is as pretty as a bird,
She is as happy as a bee,
She is as kind as a friend,
She is as friendly as a cat,
She is as helpful as a monkey,
She is as cute as a mouse,
She is lovelier than a chick,
She is my mum.

Libby-Mae Deller (6)
Prior Park Pre-Prep School, Cricklade

A Riddle

He is as nice as a lady,
He is as kind as a shopkeeper,
He is as good as Rooney,
His shirt is as blue as the sea,
He is as big as a giant,
He is as tame as a baby.
He is John Terry.

Ben Simmonds (6)
Prior Park Pre-Prep School, Cricklade

A Riddle

He is as naughty as a gorilla,
His hair is as orange as fire,
He is as tall as a whiteboard,
He is as cheeky as a monkey,
He is Johnny Test.

Matthew Krenik (7)
Prior Park Pre-Prep School, Cricklade

A Riddle

He is as friendly as Santa,
He is as clever as a doctor,
He is as famous as a movie star,
He is as cool as Batman,
He is as fast as a jaguar,
He is Frank Lampard.

Ivan Lok (6)
Prior Park Pre-Prep School, Cricklade

A Riddle

He is as cheeky as a monkey,
He is as funny as a clown,
He is as scary as a ghost,
He is as handsome as a prince,
He is as friendly as my dad,
He is as loving as my mum,
He is my brother, Leo.

Kimberley Mok (7)
Prior Park Pre-Prep School, Cricklade

What Am I?

I am very small,
I have a short tail,
I have brown fur,
I have a cage,
I eat biscuits,
What am I?
I am a hamster.

Bethany Berry (7)
Ramsbury Primary School, Ramsbury

What Am I?

I kick,
I munch,
I have four legs,
I jump,
I run,
I have long legs,
I have big ears,
I am a horse.

Eleanor Foale (6)
Ramsbury Primary School, Ramsbury

Who Am I?

I have whiskers,
I pounce for milk,
I like mice,
I have small ears,
I'm fluffy and white,
I have toys,
I go to sleep in the day,
I go out at night to nibble mice,
I like water,
I have small eyes,
I have a red tongue,
I have a collar,
I walk at night,
My name is Spotty,
I like to run,
I like biscuits,
I have a basket to sleep,
I try to play the piano,
I'll pounce if you're bad,
I have silky ears.
I'm a cat.

Joel Davies (7)
Ramsbury Primary School, Ramsbury

What Am I?

I sleep anywhere,
I eat biscuits,
I have my own bed,
I have whiskers,
I have a short tail,
I have green eyes,
I drink water,
My eyes glow in the dark,
I don't like getting wet,
I have a red tongue,
I eat meat,
I have sharp claws and I make holes with them,
I have paws,
I have a pink nose,
I have small eyes,
My name is Tootsie,
I have a brother called Blewie,
I have fur,
I scratch furniture,
I can climb trees,
I miaow.
I am a cat.

Sebastian Crawford (7)
Ramsbury Primary School, Ramsbury

What Am I?

I am spotty.
I eat flies,
I like the shade,
I sleep on the African rocks,
I stick to everything,
I stick to trees,
I like it inside houses.
I am a gecko.

Mia Kuramoto (6)
Ramsbury Primary School, Ramsbury

What Am I?

I leap in the water,
I'm mostly blue,
I've got a pointy tail,
I'm lively sometimes,
I've got fins,
They have smooth skin,
I squeak a lot,
I am a dolphin.

Josie Banovic (6)
Ramsbury Primary School, Ramsbury

What Am I?

I have soft ears,
I eat biscuits,
I sleep a lot,
I have a long tail,
I have whiskers,
I eat meat,
I have paws,
I purr,
I make holes in the furniture,
I am a cat.

Harry Bailey (7)
Ramsbury Primary School, Ramsbury

What Am I?

I bite and scratch.
I am furry and mean,
I can run fast,
I have sharp teeth,
I have a long mane,
I am a lion.

Oliver Lillywhite (6)
Ramsbury Primary School, Ramsbury

What Am I?

I have a collar on my neck,
I eat meat in a bowl,
I like toys in my bed,
I don't have hair at all,
I like to drink water,
I like to have long walks,
I have whiskers,
I sleep in my basket,
I go *woof, woof,*
I am quite furry,
I have sharp teeth,
I have a long tail.
I am a dog.

Kali Flett (7)
Ramsbury Primary School, Ramsbury

What Am I?

I have got better hearing than you,
I've got paws,
I go outside in the night,
I love meat and fish,
I have got a pink nose,
I go to sleep in the day,
I drink milk,
I scratch the furniture,
I have green eyes,
My eyes glow in the dark,
I eat biscuits,
I am a cat.

Tom Barker (7)
Ramsbury Primary School, Ramsbury

What Am I?

I have whiskers,
I have small ears,
I live in a cage,
I have little legs,
I am fluffy,
I have blue and green eyes,
I am a hamster.

Matthew Smith (7)
Ramsbury Primary School, Ramsbury

What Am I?

I swim
I climb trees
I carry my babies on my back
Some of us are nocturnal
Some of us have ring tails
We look like moneys
I am a lemur.

Tom Ahl (6)
Ramsbury Primary School, Ramsbury

What Am I?

I have a small tail.
I have floppy ears.
I like to hop around all day.
Do you know what I am?
I have lots of brothers and sisters
And I also have two front teeth sticking out.
What am I?
Yes, I am a bunny.

Sofia Orford (6)
Ramsbury Primary School, Ramsbury

What Am I?

I live in the jungle,
I have big ears,
I have a trunk,
I squirt water,
I walk slowly,
I am an elephant.

Eva Marsh (7)
Ramsbury Primary School, Ramsbury

What Am I?

I eat meat.
I have two ears, a tail and black spots,
I make the sound *woof!*
I am medium sized,
I eat biscuits,
I keep people safe from burglars,
I roll around,
I lie on furniture,
I have my own bed,
I am a dog.

George Wardley (6)
Ramsbury Primary School, Ramsbury

Watch Out!

My teeth are sharp,
I look scary,
I am big, like a bus,
I live in the sea.

Christopher Mundy (6)
St John's CE Primary School, Tisbury

Pineapple

I am sweeter than a monkey
I am as juicy as a pear
I am as yellow and colourful as a rainbow
I am as pretty as a butterfly
I taste sweet
I am as prickly as a beech tree
Some people love me
I get stuck in your teeth
I look like a tree.

Ella Kent (7)
St John's CE Primary School, Tisbury

Dinosaur

I feel scaly
I look scary
I am snappy
I am a dinosaur.

Elisa Hulland (6)
St John's CE Primary School, Tisbury

A Butterfly

I am pretty.
I have wings.
I drink flowers.
I am beautiful.
I am big.

Isobel Field (6)
St John's CE Primary School, Tisbury

Fairy

I feel as light as a feather,
I look as pretty as a pop star,
I eat as stunning as a queen,
I have got wings.

Ella Dunkley (6)
St John's CE Primary School, Tisbury

A Koala

You can find me in Australia.
I sleep nearly all day, like a badger,
I sleep in trees, like bats,
I am like a grey squirrel.
What am I?

Rosemary Eustace (7)
St John's CE Primary School, Tisbury

The Tiger Who Came To Tea

He has stripes on his back,
He eats in a flash,
His friend is a girl,
He has terrible teeth in his terrible jaws,
His eyes are like beads,
It is the tiger who came to tea.

Martha Stone (7)
St John's CE Primary School, Tisbury

A Tractor

I feel rusty,
I go well with mud,
I look very old,
I have a driver,
What am I?

Lucy Crosbie (7)
St John's CE Primary School, Tisbury

Untitled

He is as loyal as our Queen.
He is as gentle as a floating feather.
He is as white as falling snow.
He is as fluffy as snow.
He is as graceful as a swallow.
He is as soft as my teddy bear.
He is a swan.

Luke Brown (6)
Sharpness Primary School, Berkeley

Untitled

I am as lovely as a ballerina.
I am as beautiful as an angel.
I am as colourful as a rainbow.
I am as graceful as a beautiful princess.
I am as fluttery as a hummingbird.
I am as delicate as Snow White's mirror.
I am a butterfly.

Hannah Nelmes (6)
Sharpness Primary School, Berkeley

I Am

I am as fast as a bear.
I am as white as the snow.
I am as graceful as a feather.
I am as beautiful as a snowdrop.
I am as lovely as a ballerina.
I am a swan.

Paris Peeroo (6)
Sharpness Primary School, Berkeley

I Live In The Canal

I am as graceful as a cygnet,
I am as colourful as a rainbow,
I am as lovely as a butterfly,
I am as shiny as a diamond,
I am as slow as a tortoise,
I am a fish.

Milly Croft-Hill (6)
Sharpness Primary School, Berkeley

It Is . . .

It is as strong as dried cement
It is as delicate as glass.
It is as thin as a stick.
It is as nasty as a devil.
It is as fast as a bullet.
It is as brilliant as my teacher.
It is a fox.

Nathan Browning (6)
Sharpness Primary School, Berkeley

Untitled

She is as pretty as a snowflake.
She is as cute as a kitten.
She is as lovely as a rainbow.
She is as soft as a pillow.
She is as smooth as velvet.
She is a horse.

Holly Dorrington (5)
Sharpness Primary School, Berkeley

Untitled

It is as green as ivy,
It is as blue as the sea,
It is as shiny as glass,
It is as fast as a cheetah,
It is as smooth as silk,
It is as beautiful as a snowflake,
It is a Kingfisher.

Benjamin Matthews (6)
Sharpness Primary School, Berkeley

He Is . . .

He is as white as a polar bear
He is as beautiful as a butterfly
He is as tall as a giraffe
He is as floaty as a sailing boat
He glides like a kite in the air.
He is a swan.

Zak Woodward (5)
Sharpness Primary School, Berkeley

Untitled

I am as colourful as Joseph's technicoloured coat.
I am as fast as a super bike.
I'm as cute as my teacher,
I am as fluffy as a swan,
I am as cuddly as a teddy bear,
I am Torres, Kyle's cat.

Kyle Hewer (6)
Sharpness Primary School, Berkeley

Untitled

I am as fast as a police car,
I am as cuddly as my fluffy penguin,
I am as good as a rhinoceros,
I am as cute as a baby,
I am as fluffy as candyfloss.
I am Webley, Jack's dog.

Jack Woolams (6)
Sharpness Primary School, Berkeley

Untitled

She is as soft as fluff,
She is as cute as a baby,
She is as fluffy as a cloud,
She is as white as sheep's wool,
She is as fast as a cheetah,
She is as beautiful as a princess.
She is a swan.

Troy Campbell (5)
Sharpness Primary School, Berkeley

Untitled

It is as wet as water,
It is as slippery as ice,
It is as scaly as a dragon,
It is as beautiful as a butterfly,
It is as colourful as a rainbow.
It is a fish.

Ryan Gawenda (5)
Sharpness Primary School, Berkeley

My Cat

He is as beautiful as gold,
He is as colourful as a cheetah,
He is as bouncy as a kangaroo,
He is as fast as a rocket,
He is as delicate as a vase,
He is as fluffy as a teddy bear.
He is my cat, Funfull.

Ryan Powell (7)
Sharpness Primary School, Berkeley

William

He has silky fur,
He is white,
I feed him,
I ride him,
He is William the horse.

Jenna Sleath (5)
Sunningwell CE Primary School, Sunningwell

Lily

She is 16
She wears make-up
She plays with me
She loves crunching apples
She loves me
She is my sister, Lily.

Emily Durham (5)
Sunningwell CE Primary School, Sunningwell

Radley

He is brown and white like a colourful lollipop
He is as fluffy as a teddy
He nips like a parrot
He is as nosy as a squirrel
He loves to chew his bone
He is my dog, Radley.

Loren Williams (5)
Sunningwell CE Primary School, Sunningwell

Mrs Cook

She reads me books
She helps people learn
She is always kind
She rides her bicycle
She is the smiley Mrs Cook.

Nshira Ohemea Amotwe Appoh (5)
Sunningwell CE Primary School, Sunningwell

Pig

He is as big as a tree.
He is as black as the sky.
He is as hairy as a gorilla.
He has a tail as curly as a spring.
He is as stinky as a skunk.
He is a big pink and black pig.

Ronnie Bates (5)
Sunningwell CE Primary School, Sunningwell

Loren

She is as sweet as a cat.
She loves pink like a sunset.
She smells as sweet as flowers.
She is as beautiful as a princess.
She is as ticklish as a feather.
She is as playful as a kitten.
She is as delicious as a chocolate.
She is my best friend, Loren.

Louise Bowers (5)
Sunningwell CE Primary School, Sunningwell

Archie

He has teeth as white as snow.
He is as tiny as a badger.
He is likeable.
He is Archie, my baby cousin.

Charlie Thompson (5)
Sunningwell CE Primary School, Sunningwell

Alfie

He is kind.
He has ginger hair.
He is my friend.
He is a boy.
He is Alfie.

Livai Tikoilepanoni (5)
Sunningwell CE Primary School, Sunningwell

Dad

He has tattoos.
He has a motorbike.
He loves music.
He is hairy like a monkey.
He plays with me a lot.
He is my dad.

Harry Watkinson (5)
Sunningwell CE Primary School, Sunningwell

Georgie

She likes Sylvanians.
She likes gym.
She can do a front flip.
She likes grapes.
She has yellow hair like the sun.
She is my sister, Georgie.

Imogen Nutt (5)
Sunningwell CE Primary School, Sunningwell

Mickey

He is as cute as a big ted.
He is as fast as a cheetah.
He is as noisy as a chimpanzee.
He is as small as a twig.
He is as funny as a circus.
He is Mickey the hamster.

Alfie Thompson (5)
Sunningwell CE Primary School, Sunningwell

Marmite

He is cute and cheeky.
He is friendly.
He is as black as a bat.
He follows me to school.
He is Marmite, my cat.

Shannah Dunne (5)
Sunningwell CE Primary School, Sunningwell

Miss Dodson

She is very pretty like a princess.
She likes gingerbread.
She is happy.
She is the colour of the sunset.
She is Miss Dodson.

Eugenie Norris (6)
Sunningwell CE Primary School, Sunningwell

My Daddy

He like fish
He likes playing with me
He likes the garden
He likes the park
He is my daddy.

Kimberley Pritchard (6)
Sunningwell CE Primary School, Sunningwell

1111

Goldie The Goldfish

He is as round as a tank.
He is as orange as an orange.
His mouth is as big as an apple.
He swims like a dolphin.
He is Goldie the goldfish.

Alfie William Ward Stanton (6)
Sunningwell CE Primary School, Sunningwell

Untitled

She glitters like ice on the ground.
She is magical like a shining star.
She is as beautiful as a red rose.
She flies like a fluttering butterfly.
She is as tiny as a mouse.
She has a friend called Peter Pan.
She is Tinkerbell.

Danielle Blood & Holly-Mae Bell (6)
The Avenue School, Warminster

Untitled

She is kind and her skin is like butterfly wings.
She is as pretty as a magical rainbow.
She loves a handsome prince.
She is lovely, like a bright yellow sunflower.
She has seven friends as tiny as mice.
She is Snow White.

Rhona Hocquard-Drake & Regan Rai (6)
The Avenue School, Warminster

Untitled

He is as fearsome as a lion.
He has claws as sharp as needles.
He is as quiet as a mouse when he sneaks up on little girls.
He is as tall as a tree.
He eats girls in red and grannies as tough as old boots.
He is as grey as a thundercloud.
He gets cut in half like an apple.
He is the Big Bad Wolf.

Joshua Foreman (6)
The Avenue School, Warminster

Untitled

He is as round as a smooth chicken egg.
He sits on a wall as cold as ice cubes.
He falls off the wall like a stone falling to the ground.
He is Humpty Dumpty.

Harry Clark (6)
The Avenue School, Warminster

Untitled

She is as pretty as a rainbow.
She has two evil sisters who are ugly as a troll.
Her clothes are dusty and old as rags.
She has a fairy godmother as wonderful as diamonds.
She has a glass slipper as glittering as the stars.
She is Cinderella.

Prerana Thada Magar (6)
The Avenue School, Warminster

Untitled

She is as beautiful as a model.
She is as kind as a butterfly.
She is as loving as a princess.
She is as hard working as a tired cleaner.
She is Cinderella.

Tia Williams (6)
The Avenue School, Warminster

Untitled

He is as kind as a nice, funny monkey.
He is as fun as a smiling giraffe.
He is as cool as a lovely dolphin.
He is as fast as a crawling cheetah.
He is as sweet as an elephant.
He is Steven Gerrard.

Leo Eglin (6)
The Avenue School, Warminster

Untitled

She is as lovely as a big round world
She is as beautiful as a fluttering bird
She is as kind as a soft kitten
She is as helpful as God
She is Cinderella.

Chelsea Eckert-Daniels (7)
The Avenue School, Warminster

Untitled

It is as fluffy as a cute cat.
It has sharp horns like a big elephant.
It is as dangerous as a snapping crocodile.
It is as big as a barking dog.
It is as strong as a leaping cheetah.
It has giant feet like a big cat.
It is a mammoth.

Joshua Hollis (7)
The Avenue School, Warminster

Untitled

He is as fast as a big slithering shark
He is as kind as my beautiful mum
He is as helpful as a playful kid
He is as loving as my wonderful brother
He is Indiana Jones.

Brandon Tieman (6)
The Avenue School, Warminster

Untitled

He is as dangerous as a jellyfish
He is as sneaky as a slithering snake
He is as clever as my teacher
He catches his food as quick as the whistling wind
He is as camel spider.

Logan Charlesworth (6)
The Avenue School, Warminster

Untitled

She is as beautiful as a horse
She is as lovely as a penguin
She is as wonderful as a flower
She is as colourful as a rainbow
She is my mum.

Jack Glasson (7)
The Avenue School, Warminster

Untitled

He is as kind as a colourful butterfly
He is as fast as a spotty leopard
He has two kind and caring friends
He is as short as a newborn fluffy penguin
He is Round from Indiana Jones.

Connor Carr-George (6)
The Avenue School, Warminster

It Is . . .

It is bigger than a gigantic tree
It is longer than a great white shark
It is as cute as a lion cub
It is as lovely as a fluffy kitten
It is longer than an elephant's leg
It is a giraffe.

Peter Lister (6)
The Avenue School, Warminster

It Is . . .

It is as lovely as the beautiful Cinderella
It is as soft as a cuddly person
It is as kind as a friendly crocodile
It is as helpful as a fluffy cat
It is as wonderful as a mysterious rhino
It is as kind as a stripy tiger
It is as beautiful as a singing bird
It is a dog.

Kimberley Russell (7)
The Avenue School, Warminster

He Is . . .

He is as horrid as an alligator.
He is as unhelpful as my younger brother.
He always has to be sent to his room.
He is always nasty to Peter.
He always shouts, 'Noooooo!'
He is Horrid Henry.

Matthew Prudence (7)
The Avenue School, Warminster

Untitled

She is as fabulous as Hannah Montana.
She is as beautiful as my sister.
She is as sensitive as a girl rhino.
She is as helpful as a spider.
She is as loving as my friend.
She is as kind as a deer.
She is beautiful Cinderella.

Nicole Pugh (6)
The Avenue School, Warminster

Who Is He?

He sells a cow as stripy as a zebra.
He buys special beans as magic as the stars.
He grows a beanstalk as tall as a giraffe.
He meets a giant as angry as a wolf.
He is Jack from 'Jack and the Beanstalk'.

Camron Fraser & Joshua Jacques (6)
The Avenue School, Warminster

Untitled

She is as pretty as the glistening sun.
She has a witch for a stepmother who's as wicked as a monster.
She gets trapped in a tower as tall as a skyscraper.
She has shiny, golden hair that is longer than a winding river.
She married a handsome prince.
She is Rapunzel.

Jasmin Fitzgibbon (6)
The Avenue School, Warminster

Untitled

She is as pretty as a rainbow.
She is as kind as a special friend.
She wears clothes as dirty as dusty rags.
She lives with her sisters as ugly as goo.
She wears a shiny glass slipper that sparkles like the stars.
She is Cinderella.

Connor Gale (6)
The Avenue School, Warminster

Untitled

She has a pretty cloak as red as a tomato.
She has long dark hair that shines like the sun.
She skips through the creepy woods like a beautiful ballerina.
She is followed by a bad wolf that has teeth as sharp as needles.
She is Little Red Riding hood.

Charlotte Hill (6)
The Avenue School, Warminster

Untitled

She is as beautiful as a spring flower.
She is as kind as a butterfly.
Her skin is as soft as a pillow.
She eats an apple as poisonous as a snake.
She sleeps like a baby.
A prince kisses her cheek as rosy as a ruby.
She is Snow White.

Sarah-Jayne Lacey & Ella Low (6)
The Avenue School, Warminster

Untitled

He is as bad as a troll.
He is as cross as a mad monster.
He is as nasty as a crocodile.
His home is the forest as dark as the night sky.
He likes to scare a young boy called Peter.
His fur is as grey as stone.
He is the wolf from 'Peter and the Wolf'.

Kieran Mundy (6)
The Avenue School, Warminster

Untitled

She is as beautiful as a bright, yellow sunflower.
She is as pretty as a colourful rainbow.
She dances like a butterfly.
She is kind and helpful like my mummy.
She is lovelier than the stars.
She dances with a beast as tall as a giraffe.
She is Belle from Beauty and the Beast.

Caitlyn Newble (5)
The Avenue School, Warminster

Untitled

He is as ugly as a big, fat troll.
He likes eating grannies as old as dinosaurs.
His fur is as grey as an elephant.
His teeth are as sharp as pins.
His teeth are as sharp as the night sky.
He is the Big, Bad Wolf.

Taylor Bond (5)
The Avenue School, Warminster

Untitled

She has a cloak as red as roses.
She hops through the woods like a jumping kangaroo.
She meets a wolf with teeth as sharp as razors.
She is Little Red Riding Hood.

Finley Pomeroy (6)
The Avenue School, Warminster

Untitled

He is as round as a bowling ball.
He sits on a wall as tall as a tree.
He falls and cracks his head like an egg falling from a nest.
The King's men arrive as fast as a racing car.
He is Humpty Dumpty.

Owen Cressey (6)
The Avenue School, Warminster

Untitled

She is as kind as a happy cat
She is as lovely as a golden fish
She is as beautiful as a cheeky monkey
She is as fabulous as a strong tiger.
She is Cinderella.

Rachel Craft (6)
The Avenue School, Warminster

Ruby

She is as orange as the bright glistening sun.
She is as funny as Miss Rogers.
She is as gorgeous as Cinderella.
She is as playful as my special dad.
She is my cat, Ruby.

Katie Clarke (6)
The Avenue School, Warminster

My Toy

It is as fast as a bright blue dolphin.
It is as strong as sparkling clump of diamonds.
It is as bouncy as a piece of crumply paper.
It is as colourful as a rainbow of paint.
It is a Bakugan.

Tom McGavin (6)
The Avenue School, Warminster

Untitled

It jumps like a frog and really high.
It can be any colour and bold.
It is very fluffy and soft and smooth.
It leaps like a ballerina.
It has whiskers like string.
It is quiet when it walks.
It is my cat, Amber.

Jessica Johnson (7)
The Avenue School, Warminster

Untitled

He is as lazy as a sleeping baby.
He is as happy as a child playing outside.
He is as naughty as a teenager.
He is as excited as a toddler every day.
He is Robin Martin from X Factor.

Lucy Sutcliffe (6)
The Avenue School, Warminster

Rapunzel

She has hair as shiny as the golden sun.
Her hair is as long as a ribbon blowing in the wind.
She is as beautiful as a spring flower.
She was locked in a tower as tall as a tree.
She was rescued by a prince as brave as a soldier.
She is Rapunzel.

Miller Reid (5)
The Avenue School, Warminster

A Wonderful Dress

She is as beautiful as a crown.
She is as nice as the sun.
She wears a beautiful dress.
A wonderful dress.
She marries a prince.

Billy Copeland & Christopher Tukeba Bevu (5)
The Avenue School, Warminster

Love

He is in love.
He was handsome but he got beautiful.
He has a trusted stead.
He is Prince Charming.

Hayden Cuss (5)
The Avenue School, Warminster

Beautiful

She is beautiful.
She is happy.
She is pretty.
She has a glass slipper.
She is ginormous.
She is precious.
She is Cinderella.

Jamie Lee (6) & Samantha J Sargent (5)
The Avenue School, Warminster

As A Star

She is as beautiful as a star.
She is as nice as a chair.
She is Cinderella.

Harry Collins (5)
The Avenue School, Warminster

The Sky

Her dress is as beautiful as her hair.
She is like the sky.
Her dress is like the sun.
She is Cinderella.

Michael Hayward (5) & Marshall Miller (6)
The Avenue School, Warminster

She Is Beautiful

She is beautiful.
She is good and she is funny.
She has a shiny slipper.
She is as beautiful as the stars.
She is Cinderella.

Patty Stanowska & Megan Pulay (5)
The Avenue School, Warminster

Shooting Star

She is as nice as a crown.
She dances like a shooting star.
She is as pretty as the Fairy Godmother.
She goes to a ball.
She is Cinderella.

Bobby Webb & Hayden Cuss (5)
The Avenue School, Warminster

Cinderella

She is caring like a mother.
She is as beautiful as the sun.
She shimmers like the moon.
She is as pretty as the stars.
Her dress is as dirty as old, muddy puddles.
Her dress is thread-bare.
It can be gold like the moon.
She is Cinderella.

Ellie Morgan & Tawana Jaricha (5)
The Avenue School, Warminster

Cinderella

She is as beautiful as diamonds.
She is as nice as the stars.
She is as caring as can be.
She is Cinderella.

Jordan Collyer & Hayley McGavin (5)
The Avenue School, Warminster

Cinderella

She is as beautiful as the sun.
She is as caring as Mummy.
Her dress is gold like a cross in a church.
She marries a prince.
She is as lovely as the moon.
She is Cinderella.

George Wrenn & Charlie Lloyd-Owens (6)
The Avenue School, Warminster

Red As A Heart

She is as red as a heart.
She has a basket.
She has in her basket some flowers.
She was in the woods.
She is Little Red Riding Hood.

Bailey Griffin (6)
The Avenue School, Warminster

Gold Like The Stars

She is as pretty as the moon.
She is as gold as the stars.
She is as beautiful as a heart.
She has a glass slipper.
It is Cinderella.

Marshall-Lee Bond (5) & Bailey Griffin (6)
The Avenue School, Warminster

My Cat Ollie

It is as funny as a juggler,
It is as smiley as an elephant,
It is as silly as a kangaroo,
It is as bouncy as a squirrel,
It is as cuddly as a teddy,
It is my cat, Ollie.

Grace Garner (6)
Woodborough CE (A) Primary School, Woodborough

Untitled

She is as smiley as a clown,
She is as clever as an artist,
She is as rich as a bank,
She is as fast as a cheetah,
She is as bossy as a teacher,
She is as colourful as a rainbow,
She is the Queen.

Louis Cartwright
Woodborough CE (A) Primary School, Woodborough

She Is . . .

She is as tuneful as a singer,
She is as pretty as a flower,
She is as sparkly as a sequin,
She is as happy as a clown,
She is as smiley as Miley,
She is Hannah Montana.

Sian Drew (6)
Woodborough CE (A) Primary School, Woodborough

Untitled

He is as funny as a clown,
He is as happy as a cheetah,
He is as cool as a king,
He is as nice as Henry,
He is William G.

Charlie Britten
Woodborough CE (A) Primary School, Woodborough

My Teacher

She is as bossy as Lucy S,
She is as cheeky as a chick,
She is as colourful as a peacock,
She is as cute as a flower,
She is as big as an elephant,
She is smaller than a tree,
She is as good as me,
She is as busy as can be,
She is as funny as me,
She is as crazy as me,
She is as cool as a cat.
She is Mrs Barratt, my teacher.

Natasha Speechley (5)
Woodborough CE (A) Primary School, Woodborough

119

Untitled

He is as brave as a female T-rex.
He is as kind as Jesus.
He is as charming as a boy.
He is as happy as a queen.
He is as funny as a teacher.
He is a prince.

Henry Vigor (5)
Woodborough CE (A) Primary School, Woodborough

She Is . . .

She is as pretty as a ring,
She has hair like a giraffe,
She is as rich as Jesus,
She is as skinny as a stick insect,
She is as small as a mouse,
She is a princess.

Henry Willis (6)
Woodborough CE (A) Primary School, Woodborough

That's Me

He is as silly as a monkey,
He is as quick as a cheetah,
He is as playful as a dog,
He is as kind as a rabbit,
He is as cheerful as a lion,
He is Sean, that's me.

Sean Montgomery (6)
Woodborough CE (A) Primary School, Woodborough

He Is . . . Regie

He is as fluffy as a cloud,
He is as fat as a crocodile,
He is as big as a monkey,
He is as peaceful as a bird,
He's as happy as a dog,
He's my cockerel.

Honor Petitt (6)
Woodborough CE (A) Primary School, Woodborough

Untitled

He is as bouncy as a kangaroo,
He is as fluffy as wavy grass,
He is as nibbly as a squirrel,
He is as fast as a leopard,
He is my rabbit.

Jonathan Trowbridge
Woodborough CE (A) Primary School, Woodborough

MJ

He's as scary as the top of a skyscraper,
He's as cool as a cool boy,
He's as rich as JLS,
He's as funny as a clown,
He's as intelligent as a pencil,
He's Michael Jackson.

Devon Rookes (6)
Woodborough CE (A) Primary School, Woodborough

Lucy's Riddle

It is as furry as a tiger,
It is as bouncy as a bunny,
It is as silly as a monkey,
It is as sweet as a kitten,
It has a black collar,
It is my dog.

Lucy Stevenson (6)
Woodborough CE (A) Primary School, Woodborough

Charlie

He is as playful as a ball,
He is as fluffy as a cloud,
He is as scruffy as a beard,
He is as cute as my face,
He is as fast as a race horse,
He is my puppy, Charlie.

Lucy Tyler (7)
Woodborough CE (A) Primary School, Woodborough

My Best Friend

He is as kind as a teacher
He is as good as a man
He is as good as God
He is as kind as your dad
He is as kind as your sister
He is Henry Barker.

Robert Herrett (6)
Woodborough CE (A) Primary School, Woodborough

Untitled

It is as blonde as a chick
It is as humpy as a camel
It is as lumpy as chickenpox
It is as furry as a chihuahua
It is as furry as a chick
It is a camel.

Clementine Woodard
Woodborough CE (A) Primary School, Woodborough

She Is . . .

She is as funny as a clown
She is as cute as a bunny
She is as nice as a monkey
She is as careful as a mouse
She is as playful as a cat
She is my mum.

William Ford (6)
Woodborough CE (A) Primary School, Woodborough

Young Writers Information

We hope you have enjoyed reading this book - and that you will continue to enjoy it in the coming years. If you like reading and writing poetry drop us a line, or give us a call, and we'll send you a free information pack. Alternatively if you would like to order further copies of this book or any of our other titles, then please give us a call or log onto our website at www.youngwriters.co.uk.

Young Writers Information
Remus House
Coltsfoot Drive
Peterborough
PE2 9JX
(01733) 890066